THE HITMAN'S REDEMPTION

A SUNSET COAST BOOK

SADIE KING

THE HITMAN'S REDEMPTION

You always remember your first hit. But you don't expect to fall for his daughter...

For twelve years, I've been haunted by the girl with blue eyes flecked with amber. The girl who witnessed my first hit.

When our paths unexpectedly cross, I know I'll do whatever it takes to get close to her, even if it means pretending to be someone else. Someone better.

She must never know I'm the one who killed her father...

The Hitman's Redemption is Sting and Liberty's story, a sweet stalker, OTT instalove romance with a flawed hero and a curvy heroine who may just heal his heart.

There's plenty of steam, no cliffhangers, and a happy-ever-after guaranteed.

DON'T MISS OUT!

Want to be the first to hear about new releases and special offers?
Follow Sadie King on BookBub to get an alert whenever she has a new release, preorder, or discount!

www.bookbub.com/authors/sadie-king

Copyright © 2022 by Sadie King.

All rights reserved.

No part of this book may be reproduced in any form or by any electronic or mechanical means, including information storage and retrieval systems, without written permission from the author, except for the use of brief quotations in a book review.

This is a work of fiction. Any resemblance to actual events, companies, locales or persons living or dead, are entirely coincidental.

Cover design Designrans

www.authorsadieking.com

1
STING

The butt of the rifle presses against my cheek, its sharp metallic smell reminding me of Iraq.

It reminds me of when I was crouched on sand-covered rooftops, concealed and patient, covering my platoon as they cleared another war-damaged village.

My job was to wait, and when the enemy showed up, as they often did, I was ready.

As the platoon sniper, my job was an easy one: kill the enemy before they killed my soldiers.

But I'm not in Iraq, and the person on the other end of my sight isn't my enemy. They're someone else's enemy. I'm just the hired gun. The hitman.

There're only two people I work for. Damon Fletcher, who saved me from the streets when I was a homeless army vet with no future. And my other client, Markus Johnson, who fights the war on drugs with his own brand of vigilante justice. He gives me the details, and I don't ask questions. Any scum selling drugs to vulnerable people doesn't deserve to live.

A car turns onto the street, a black Mercedes with tinted windows.

In the fading light, I can just make out the license plate. This is my guy.

A sudden breeze sends a plastic bag tripping down the street ahead of the Mercedes. It rolls across the grass and catches on the edge of a broken fence, snagging between the twisted wires.

The car pulls up outside the only dark house on the street. Other houses have rectangles of yellow light with shapes moving behind them, families finishing their dinners and kids dragging their feet on their way to bed.

It's not a wealthy neighborhood. There's graffiti on the side of a garage and a couch dumped on the sidewalk, the long grass licking its edges.

Hard working families live here. Parents doing their best for their kids while working two jobs just to put food on the table.

It's the kind of neighborhood a man like the one I'm about to kill thrives on.

He's got no business driving in here with his Mercedes, making every young man on the street look at him with envy and every mother tut as fear grips her heart.

This community will be shocked when they learn their new neighbor is—soon to be *was*—a notorious drug dealer. The house has probably already been made into a lab. It's better to get this scum out of the neighborhood.

There'll be a scandal about the shooting, and mothers will worry if their kids are safe. But they'll be a hell of a lot safer than if this dirtbag had gotten a foothold in their community.

The drugs lab is just the start. Soon it would be recruiting bored teenagers looking to make a quick buck. Then there're the free samples. It's the vulnerable people in the community

—the ones down on their luck, the ones with mental health problems, the army vets with nowhere to go, the single parents needing a few minutes of peace, the uneducated women who can only see one way to make a living and need a hit to block out their reality. Those are the ones men like this target. Those are the ones who'll pay the price if drug pushers are allowed to take hold.

The car stops, and the driver's door opens. My finger rests on the trigger of the gun. I've got to do it in the few seconds it takes him to walk from the car to his front door.

My body goes still, waiting for the right moment.

There's movement in the corner of my eye. I swing the sight around, and a girl on a bike comes into view.

What the hell is she doing out on her own in this neighborhood after dark?

She's got to be about twelve years old, her blond hair streaming out behind her as she rides.

The sound of a car door slamming snaps my attention back to the hit. He's out of the car and jingling his keys as he walks toward the house.

I've got to do it now.

The girl rides toward the man, and he turns to give her a smile. She puts her foot on the ground and stops her bike to have a few words with him.

He's in my sights. If I pulled the trigger now, I'd get him right between the eyes. A clean hit. But I'd also get blood on the girl.

My mind goes back to another hit from twelve years ago, my first hit after Damon Fletcher pulled me off the streets and gave my life a new purpose.

I hesitated then.

Pulling a trigger when you're in the army and the guy on the other end is trying to kill your soldiers is one thing. But pulling the trigger in cold blood is another.

I hesitated, and the man ran. I chased him through the house, and there was a scuffle. We both ended up on the floor in the bedroom before I got my shot, his brain matter and blood spraying all over my clothes and face.

When he went still, there was a set of eyes watching me. A girl, about twelve years old, her eyes wide in shock, her pretty face splattered with blood.

I stared at her and she stared back, her dark eyes round and terrified.

There wasn't meant to be anyone else in the house. The intel Damon told me was wrong. I knew what he'd want me to do. He'd want me to tie up loose ends, to eliminate the girl.

But as we stared at each other, her eyes wide in terror, I knew in a heartbeat that I wouldn't harm her.

I pressed my fingers to my lips. "Shhh," I said.

The girl watched me, the terror giving way to curiosity. Her eyes were blue, with a fleck of amber in the left eye.

She started that day as a regular kid, probably thinking about what ribbon to wear in her hair and what music to play while getting ready for school. She ended that day with the blood of who I assumed was her father splattered across her face. Her life would never be the same again.

She grew up that day, whoever she was. I may have taken her father's life, but I took that girl's innocence. And that haunts me every single day, more than the numerous kills I've done since.

I won't do that to another little girl.

My finger eases off the trigger.

I don't know what she's talking to her new neighbor about, but I'm prepared to jump down there if he tries anything with her.

He smiles benevolently at the girl and reaches into his pocket. He pulls out a piece of candy, and her eyes light up as she takes it.

Didn't anyone warn her about taking candy from strangers?

The girl stuffs the candy into her mouth and gets back on the bike. She rides off, and the hit watches her as she turns into a driveway a few houses down.

He's got a sleazy smile on his face that makes me think there's another good reason for getting rid of this scumbag. No one should look at a little girl that way.

The girl dumps her bike in the front yard and pulls open the door. I hear gentle scolding from a woman inside. She's being chastised for getting home late, but at least she won't witness a murder tonight.

My target turns and begins to walk to his front door. I follow him with my crosshairs. As soon as I hear the door shut behind the girl, I pull the trigger.

2
LIBERTY

The murmur of voices and the tinkle of champagne glasses can be heard over the jazz band playing soft welcoming music from the temporary stage in the back garden.

The straps of my dress dig into my shoulders. I tug at them, trying to adjust the position of the neckline so it covers my cleavage.

"Stop fussing." Mom's voice has a sharp edge to it as she talks out the side of her painted smile.

I take the warning and leave the dress alone, knowing I'll spend all afternoon worried that it's too tight for my oversized breasts.

It was the only dress in the secondhand shop I could squeeze into that was nice enough for the annual Fletcher garden party.

It's pale green with a high waist that shows off more of my curves than I'd like. Usually, I'd never wear something so revealing, but Mom loves it and today is all for Mom.

If she's nervous walking into the property of Damon

Fletcher, the richest man on the Sunset Coast, then she doesn't show it.

She looks good in a tailored two-piece with a single gold chain around her neck and matching understated earrings.

She doesn't look like some of the guests we pass on our way into the party, showing off their wealth with ostentatious jewelry and designer purses.

Mom looks elegant and like she belongs. No one would ever know she lives paycheck to paycheck doing accounts for small businesses and sharing her one-bedroom apartment with her three cats.

A waiter stops so we can take two drinks off his tray, and I sip the champagne slowly, enjoying the fizzy taste on my tongue.

"Don't drink too much," Mom hisses.

I refrain from rolling my eyes. Sometimes Mom forgets I'm a grown-up twenty-four-year-old and not a wayward teenager.

"Ah, here you are."

The booming voice jolts me, and I swallow too much champagne. The bubbles tickle my throat, and I cover my mouth as I try to cough quietly without embarrassing my mother.

The booming voice belongs to Damon Fletcher. He's got an appraising grin on his face as he takes my mother by both of her hands.

"Deborah. You look more and more stunning every year."

My mother coos softly and lowers her eyelashes like she's a demure teenager and not the middle-aged battle axe I know she is.

"Thank you, darling. You're too kind."

Damon turns his attention to me and gives a low whistle.

"Liberty, you're almost as pretty as your mother in that dress."

I know he's being kind, and I know complimenting a woman on her physical appearance is what men of his age do. But I'm of the generation of women who want to be seen as more than the dress they're wearing and a pair of tits.

I'm about to give a curt retort when I catch my mother's eye. She's giving me a steady look, probably terrified that I'm about to embarrass her.

I can almost hear her voice. *"Back in my day, when a man gave you a compliment, you smiled and said thank you."*

I swallow the retort and turn my scowl into a smile.

"Thank you," is all I manage to get out.

Damon smiles and thankfully his gaze doesn't linger on my body. At least he's not one of those men.

"How's the center going?"

My mind goes to the sessions from yesterday. I had a group dealing with losing someone after a long-term illness. It's different from the group dealing with losing someone suddenly. A different kind of grief. A different range of emotions.

"It's good."

Damon raises his eyebrows because no grief counseling center can really be described as good. He's looking at me expectantly, and I guess that as the main financial backer he probably wants concrete details.

"We helped one hundred and fifteen people through the center last month. I've currently got fourteen sessions running a week, and we extended the phone line hours so it's a twenty-four-hour service."

"Good. I'm glad there are people like you in our community, Liberty. What you're doing with the center is important work. You're touching people's lives. I'm very happy to keep donating."

"Thank you."

This time I mean it. We couldn't operate without

Damon's backing. I may be the one touching lives, but he's the one who makes it possible.

He turns his attention to my mom, and I use the opportunity to sneak off.

I'm grateful to Damon, but I still find the man a little creepy, like he'd do anything to keep his business interests running.

Across the garden I see Trinity, Damon's daughter, and I head over to say hi.

"Liberty!" She gives me a generous hug, only I can't get my arms around her due to the protruding belly.

Mom told me all about Trinity running off and coming back knocked up and engaged to one of Damon's men. He must have been furious.

But Trinity looks happier than I've ever seen her.

"When are you due?"

"Two more months." She rubs her tummy proudly. I feel a pang of jealousy. I've never had any luck with men.

Trinity fills me in on her husband, Karl, and the strange story of how they met. It's like a romance novel with bizarre twists and turns, and it leaves me wondering if I'll ever meet anyone that loves me that much.

I finish my drink and wander through the garden, talking to people I recognize who I only ever see once a year at the Fletcher garden party.

It's an hour later when I find Mom in the kitchen, her head thrown back in laughter at something Angela, Damon's wife, is saying.

The two women are leaning on the bench, a bottle of champagne between them, their lipstick-stained glasses half empty.

Angela sees me and steps out from around the bench, her arms wide to embrace me in a hug.

"You get prettier every time I see you, sweetheart."

She smells like caviar and an expensive scent. Angela and my mother used to be best friends. We spent a lot of time with the Fletchers when I was younger. Before everything changed.

It's good to see Mom laughing, but I desperately want to get home. I've got prep I need to do for work tomorrow. I've got client notes to write up, and I need to look over my notes for my first session of the day.

"I'm gonna go, Mom. I can find my own way home."

"Are you sure, love? It's still early."

It's so rare to see Mom laughing. I don't want to drag her away.

"I've got work to do. I can get a bus."

Mom winces, and I realize I've said the wrong thing. We're probably the only guests here who don't have a fleet of cars waiting to chauffeur us around. Like we used to.

"A bus?" Angela exclaims. "Don't be silly, dear. We'll get one of our men to drive you home."

There's no use protesting, and I don't want to make Mom feel even more awkward.

Angela goes in search of "one of her men," and a few minutes later she's ushering me toward a black station wagon.

I say my goodbyes, and even though it's been nice to see some old friends, I feel relief flood me as I leave the property. The Fletcher world is not one where I belong anymore.

I'm too embarrassed to give the address of the rundown apartment where I live, so I tell the driver to drop me off in the nice part of town.

It's a bit of a drive inland from the coast, and it's almost twilight when the car pulls up outside of the fake address.

As soon as the car's out of sight, I head to the bus stop to catch a ride across town.

3
STING

The cool air hits the back of my neck, and I pull my coat tight around myself, sealing off the elements. My hands are jammed into my pockets as I walk the quiet streets.

The hit was two days ago. For two days I've had a feeling of unease in the pit of my stomach. Maybe it was seeing the little girl that reminded me of that first hit so many years ago. Maybe it was seeing the bullet enter the man's head, sending brain matter out of his own skull.

Usually, I do the job and never think about it again. But this time, I can't forget.

A blast of cold air sends a stab of pain through my shoulder. I rotate the joint, trying to ease the ache, but the old injury is playing up.

It's the reason I was discharged from the army. A bullet went into my shoulder. It came straight out the other side but left me with a faulty joint.

I pleaded not to be discharged. I begged them to go back to war, to the only thing in my life where I ever felt like I belonged. But that seemed to make them more convinced that I needed out.

I was discharged with nowhere to go, no family, and no job prospects. There were community assimilation programs and recruitment drives, but those programs are no good for a man like me.

I was lost before I joined the army. I went back to being lost afterwards.

A bus goes past, kicking up leaves and litter, making them swirl in the gutter. It slows down at the bus stop, and the thick doors creak open.

I think about getting on, going home, and getting comfortable with a microwave meal and a six pack of beer. But tonight, I want to walk.

A woman gets off the bus. She's got a shawl pulled around her shoulders, covering up a satin green dress. The luscious fabric swirls around her knees. It's not the kind of dress anyone who needs to take the bus wears.

The satin is pulled tight around her curvy ass, which sways as she walks away from the bus stop. My gaze travels up the smooth legs, the round ass, the straight back, and the long neck held proud and tall. Wisps of blond hair trail over her neck, having fallen down from the bun on top of her head. Her hair, catching in the streetlight, looks like a halo. My very own angel.

I long to run my hand over her smooth neck and scoop the hair off her skin.

My breathing gets heavy, and my heartbeat goes up a notch. I fall into step behind the woman and, without realizing what I'm doing, follow her down the street.

She walks confidently, her low-heeled sandals making clicking sounds on the pavement. I wonder who she is, where she's been, and who the hell lets her walk around town when it's almost dark.

THE HITMAN'S REDEMPTION

My fists clench. If she was my woman, I wouldn't let her walk around on her own at night.

When she's my woman, I'll never leave her side.

The thought hits me like a jolt in the heart.

This is my woman.

She is mine.

I can tell from the way she carries herself that she's good and kind and confident. I can tell from the sway of her ass that she's everything a man needs. The delicate curve of her neck shows me her vulnerability.

How I'd love to put my hands around her neck as I thrust into her, making her scream my name as she comes.

I stop in the shadows and lean against the wall. With my hands on my knees, I take deep breaths, wondering what the hell I'm doing.

There's a vulnerable young woman walking on her own, and I'm having dirty thoughts about her. If she looked back, if she saw me following her, she'd report me to the police.

She doesn't know that I'm protecting her, that I'm making sure she gets home safe.

I straighten up and follow from a safe distance. I don't want her to know I'm here. Not yet.

The woman turns onto a street with two tall apartment buildings. I dart across the road and into an alleyway.

Keeping to the shadows, I pull out my field binoculars to get a better look at my angel.

I trail the binoculars up her body, from the small of her back to the back of her neck. She's standing in a pool of light. My angel. Before she goes into the building, she turns slightly, and I see her face for the first time.

I gasp and stagger backwards. My angel with the pale neck and golden hair has blue eyes, the left one with a fleck of amber. I'd recognize those eyes anywhere. They're the eyes that have haunted my dreams for the last twelve years.

4
LIBERTY

The hair on the back of my neck stands on end. I've felt this way ever since I got off the bus a few blocks away.

I turn quickly and survey the street. But there's no one around.

A shiver goes down my spine, and I get a dizzying feeling, like déjà vu.

It must be the champagne. I had two glasses, and the only food I had was those tiny canapes. There's a frozen pizza in the freezer, and I'm going to get that in the oven as soon as I get upstairs.

Without another thought about it, I open the door and head up to my apartment.

It's a small one-bedroom, and the rent is almost my entire take-home pay, but it's worth it to have my own space. Living with my mom was great, but there comes a time in a girl's life where she's got to get out from living with her mother.

We still talk most days and I visit her a few times a week.

But coming home to my own place at the end of a long day is a comfort I'm willing to pay for.

Especially with the work that I do. I've created my own rituals for the end of the day, leaving the emotion at work and keeping my home an emotionally safe space.

I light one scented candle at the front door and one in the living room. It's sandalwood, meant to rebalance and soothe. One of my self-care rituals.

While the pizza's heating up, I pull out the case work I need to catch up on. It doesn't take me long to write up the notes from today's sessions.

Then I look over my client list for tomorrow. I do one-on-one client sessions which pay my rent, but it's the group sessions I live for.

They're free to attend and open to anyone, so we get a lot of people who can't access help otherwise. It's what gets me up in the mornings, knowing that I'll help someone work through their grief and make their life a little bit easier.

The pizza is deliciously greasy, and I savor every bite. My notes are covered with grease by the time I'm done.

I run a bath as I finish my pizza. A bath is another one of my self-care rituals. Every night without fail, I soak in the tub.

There's a window in the bathroom. If I leave it open, I can sit in my bath while looking at the town below and the stars above. It's not much, but it's enough to remind me there's beauty in this hard world. And with the work that I do, I need that reminder every single day.

As I sink into the warm water, surrounded by bubbles with the scent of lavender oil, I close my eyes and let my body relax.

5

STING

My hands clench around the steaming flask as I let the warmth seep into my bones. In the pre-dawn light, I can just make out the tendrils of steam that snake into the air. I take a sip, feeling the burning coffee warm me up from the inside out.

From my position in the service entrance of the apartment building opposite Liberty's, I have a clear view of the entrance to her apartment building.

I know her name now. It didn't take much digging to find out the name of the daughter of my first hit. Liberty Jones.

Her father had some business dealings with Damon Fletcher that went bad. I don't know the details. I don't need to know. All I know is his daughter is in the apartment across the road. The girl that has haunted my dreams for the last twelve years is now a fully grown woman.

I got here early in case she's an early jogger or a shift worker. But so far the only person I've seen come out of the building was a woman in a party dress, her high heels dangling from one hand, doing the walk of shame.

I'm still wondering what weird coincidence put Liberty

Jones in my path last night. It must be fate pushing us together.

There's movement across the road, and Liberty emerges from her apartment building. I lift my binoculars to my eyes to get a better look.

She's wearing a light-blue checkered top that hangs low over black leggings that hug her curvy thighs. Her blonde hair is tied up on top of her head, strands hanging down to frame her face.

She was beautiful in her nice dress last night, but in her casual work wear, with her face unhindered by makeup, she's stunning.

I follow her with my binoculars, keeping them trained on the nape of her neck where the wispy strands of hair tickle her skin.

I wonder what she tastes like, how her skin would feel on my tongue. I bet she smells good. Milky sweet and a light perfume. She probably smells of coffee and feminine soap.

My cock thickens at the thought of her scent, at the thought of the taste of her skin and the little noises she'll make as I taste every part of her.

For now, I can only imagine, but I'll know soon enough.

Liberty turns the corner, and I emerge onto the street and follow.

It's easy to tail her in the morning rush of commuters hurrying to work. I stay half a block behind, using the chattels of the city for concealment.

Liberty walks a few blocks before taking the stairs to a rundown building. The concrete walls are stained dark at the corners. There're splashes of graffiti, and the paint is chipping off the window frames.

I don't like the idea of Liberty working in a place like this.

Following her up the stairs, I wait a beat before I push the creaky wooden door open.

Inside is a short corridor with faded carpet. There is a door on one side, and at the end of the corridor are a couple of steps leading to a waiting area. My breath hitches as I see Liberty. She's leaning against the reception counter, talking with a woman.

The woman behind the counter says something, and Liberty tilts her head back and laughs. It's a soft sound, like the burble of a trickling brook. I close my eyes, listening to the murmur of her soft voice.

I'm not ready to see Liberty yet, so I hang back in the corridor, studying the faded chalk board pinned with notices, trying to work out what goes on in this neglected building in the rough part of town.

There's a brochure for a helpline, numbers to call if you're feeling suicidal, and a pamphlet from the Salvation Army.

My gaze moves from the notice board to the yellowing sign next to it.

Grief Services
We're here to listen.

It's a counseling center. A grief counseling center.

My stomach knots at the thought that Liberty's still grieving after all these years. I did that to her.

My hand goes to my head, and I lean against the wall, closing my eyes and breathing hard. I should walk away. I should leave her alone. I'm an animal, a hitman, the scum of the earth. I've got no business poking around in Liberty's life.

"Are you okay?"

A gentle voice pulls me back from the edge. I open my eyes to find two pale blue eyes, one flecked with amber, looking at me.

Her expression is kind and concerned. She's looking at me like I'm a decent human being, like she believes there's goodness in me.

"Would you like a glass of water?"

Her genuine concern goes straight to my heart.

She thinks I've stumbled in here looking for help. She has no idea I followed her here, that I don't deserve her kindness, that I cause grief and darkness wherever I go.

"Thank you." My voice comes out hoarse.

Her gaze lingers on my face, and my heart skips a beat, wondering if she recognizes me.

"Come in and sit for a moment."

I feel a flicker of disappointment as she turns away. She doesn't remember me the way I remember her.

I look different than I did twelve years ago, when I was fresh faced and floppy haired. Twelve years in my business has taken its toll. It's no wonder she doesn't recognize my hard features, the stubble on my jaw, and my close-cropped hair flecked with silver. Why would she?

Still, I can't help but feel a pang of disappointment that I'm not as memorable to her as she is to me. Yeah, I'm a selfish asshole.

I follow Liberty down the carpeted steps to the waiting area. She fills a plastic cup from the water dispenser and hands it to me.

I sit down, and she takes the chair next to me.

"Are you here for a group session?"

I don't know what the hell she means, but I'll play along if it gets me more time with Liberty.

"Yeah."

Her gaze stays on me, and I get the feeling she's waiting for me to say more. But I've always been a man of few words.

"You're a little early. The group session isn't 'til eleven, but you're welcome to stay here as long as you need."

She puts a reassuring hand on my arm, and the contact sends a warm feeling through my body. I close my eyes briefly, savoring the moment. She must take it as a sign of my grief because when I open them again, she looks concerned.

"My first client is waiting so I need to go, but here's a number you can call if you want to talk to someone."

She hands me a card, and her fingers brush mine. There's a jolt of electricity as our skin touches. Liberty takes a quick intake of breath. Her eyes flick to mine with surprise.

I hold her gaze, not daring to breathe. My heart is in my throat, and I know she felt that connection too.

She stands up and the moment's gone, leaving me wondering if I imagined it.

"I'll see you at eleven."

As she walks past the reception desk and down the corridor, I watch her go.

Liberty's a grief counsellor. No doubt because of the grief I caused her as a child.

I feel guilty as hell. But that won't stop me from getting what I want. I'm an animal. I have no soul, no conscience.

I'll play along if that's how I get close to Liberty. I'll play the grief card if it gets me what I want. There's one thing I did learn today: Liberty smells like lavender and almonds.

6
LIBERTY

"Sometimes I go into the room and it takes me a while to realize he's not there..." Jane's voice wobbles, and she breaks off what she's saying.

There are murmurs around the room. The woman sitting next to Jane reaches out and takes her hand.

I nod sympathetically, but my eyes flick over to the man sitting directly opposite me in the circle. He's looking straight at me, his intense gaze not wavering even when I look up at him.

A jolt of energy goes down my spine, and I glance away quickly.

I'm not sure what it is about the broad-shouldered man I found in the corridor this morning, but every time I look at him, I feel heat creep through my body.

Sting is what he introduced himself as at the start of the session. Other than saying his name, he hasn't uttered a word.

That's not uncommon for someone's first grief session. I've helped hundreds of people work through their grief after losing a loved one.

It can be scary taking the first step, and it may take time for whatever brought him here to come out.

Jane has started talking again, and I try to bring my focus to her. But out of the corner of my eye I can see Sting still looking at me, his gaze taking me in, running over my body, making sweat bead on the back of my neck and my core pull in tight.

It suddenly feels very hot in this room.

I grip the sides of my chair, needing to bring myself back into balance. Leaning forward, I tilt my head so I can't see his profile and really try to focus on Jane.

She's stopped talking and the room is silent. I realize they're waiting for me to facilitate what happens next.

I swallow, hoping I didn't miss anything important in her story.

"Thank you for sharing."

Jane's crying now. Someone hands her one of the tissue boxes from the center of the circle.

"The next session is tomorrow, and I have one-on-one sessions if anyone would like to book."

We always end with affirmations, and I lead the group through them now.

Most members like to bow their heads and close their eyes as if in prayer. I do too. When I sneak a look up, Sting is watching me. He's not repeating the affirmations as he stares at me shamelessly.

My words falter, and I have to look down quickly before I lose my train of thought. I don't risk looking up again.

The session finishes, and there's the scraping of chairs and soft chatter as people start to leave. My throat's dry. I head over to the refreshments table where there's hot coffee and a plate of cookies.

I usually hang back and let the participants get the refreshments first, but right now I need to move.

I'm pouring myself a cup of coffee when I feel his presence behind me. I freeze with the coffee pot in the air. His breath blows hot on the back of my neck, making the hairs stand up. My body trembles as heat floods my panties.

I turn around slowly. Sting is right behind me.

"Can I get you some coffee?"

I hold up the pot, trying to act natural. But I feel anything but natural.

Up close I note his pale blue eyes, like a calm sea. There's stubble on his chin, and I have an urge to reach out and rake my hand over it, wondering what it would feel like to catch on my knuckles.

"I want a private session." His voice is deep and gravelly and reverberates through my body, making my knees wobble.

My heart skips a beat. It's dangerous to be alone with this man. I feel it in the very core of my being. The way his presence is doing things to my body that I can't control. The way he looks at me like he wants to rip my clothes off. The intensity of his gaze, like he wants to tear me open and see inside my very soul.

I should turn him down. I should send him to another therapist. I should walk away.

"I'll check my calendar."

But I don't. I make an appointment to see this man. Because even while my mind tells me it's the wrong thing to do, my body and soul can't refuse.

7
STING

My breath steams up the glass, and I wipe it away with my fist. I'm nine floors up across the road from Liberty's apartment watching the rectangle of light that is her bathroom window.

Darkness surrounds me, and I focus my binoculars on that sliver of light. She thinks no one can see her, but I'm watching.

I'm watching as she turns on the faucets, the room getting steamy as her bath fills. She lights candles and tips a few drops of oil into the bath.

She moves in and out of the bathroom, coming back and forth to check the water.

The anticipation makes my cock ache. I'm hard as a rock watching her bath time ritual, standing in the dark of the apartment that I rented out on short notice so I could watch Liberty.

My meeting with her today has me rattled. She's a fucking angel, helping people get through their grief. It's easy to see how she got into this line of work. The grief she went through. The grief that I inflicted.

I lower the binoculars and lean against the window, letting my breath steam up the glass. I don't deserve to be here watching this angel after what I've done. I don't deserve her kind words and concerned looks.

There's movement across the darkness. Without the binoculars, her window is a slit of light with a blurred shape moving behind it. There's a distance of darkness between us. Traffic passes on the street below, the noise carrying up the tall buildings.

I belong down there, on the street, far away from this angel. I should walk away. I should pack up my kit and leave her alone to get on with her life.

Instead, I raise the binoculars.

The bath is full, with fluffy peaks of bubbles piled high out of the water. She's standing next to the bath. As I watch, her hand goes to her shirt, and she undoes the top button.

My dick stirs, and I let out a growl, the sound echoing around the empty apartment. With each button, my dick lengthens until she's standing in her bra and my cock's straining against my jeans.

The bra's made of faded white lace, the delicate fabric encasing her breasts, caressing them. There's a hole in the fabric under her arm pit, and the lace is coming undone in places, stringing fabric tickling her skin.

It pierces my heart to see Liberty in worn underwear. She's chosen a profession that helps people, but I'm guessing it doesn't pay much.

When Liberty's my woman, she can have anything she goddamn wants. I'll buy her new lacey underwear that's suitable for my queen.

She reaches around and unhooks her bra. Her breasts tumble out of their restraint, hanging loose and heavy like glorious pillows that I long to run my dick over. Her nipples are dark peaks aching for my touch.

SADIE KING

Then she bends down and slides off her leggings.

"Holy fuck."

Liberty steps into the bath, and I get a peek of blonde bush, thick, curly hair that frames her sweet cunt.

I can imagine her pale, thick thighs straddling me as I suck on her glorious nipples.

As she slides under the water, I slide my dick out of my pants.

With one hand on the binoculars and the other on my dick, I tug with long, hard pulls. She sinks under the water, her breasts floating under the bubbles, her nipples breaking the surface like dark beacons.

Liberty closes her eyes and tilts her head back to lean on the back of the bath, exposing her soft neck.

My tugging gets harder as I stroke my cock with long steady moves from the shaft to the tip.

She picks up a cloth and rubs soapy cream up her arms and over her chest and breasts.

It's too much. My orgasm rips through me, and I shoot hot cum into my fist, imagining I'm coming all over her tits, that I'm the cream she's rubbing onto herself.

My grunts fall against the glass, muted and lonely with no one to hear them.

I'm not proud of what I've just done. I'm not proud of this obsession I have with the girl with the amber fleck in her eyes.

I'll never be the kind of man she deserves. I have a darkness in me, a gray moral compass. She deserves better than that.

For a moment, an alternate reality flashes into my mind. A reality where I have a regular job, where I work an honest day's work and our home is filled with children and Liberty's soft laugh.

My phone rings, and Damon's number flashes up.

There's only one reason Damon calls me.

I hold the phone out, letting it ring. This is my reality. This is my life. I'll never work a nine-to-five job. I'll never be the man that Liberty deserves. I wouldn't know how.

I let the phone ring a few more times before answering it. Damon's voice is crisp down the line.

"I've got a job for you."

I turn away from the window. This is my reality. You can't change who you are.

8
LIBERTY

"This is a safe space. There's no judgement here."

It's how I start every new counseling session, but the words sound hollow said to the man opposite me with the intense pale blue eyes.

My hands fidget nervously in my lap, and I thrust them under my thighs to keep them still.

I'm the counselor here. I'm the one that's meant to be easing my patient's anxiety. But instead I'm shifting in my seat while a low throb takes hold in my core.

"What brought you here today?"

I try again, but Sting doesn't say much. In some clients the hurt is so deep that it takes a long time before they can talk about it.

I wait while he watches me, his gaze making me squirm.

"My mother died."

His voice is a deep rumble that I feel all the way through my bones. It takes me a moment to realize what he's said.

"I'm sorry for your loss."

Sting's gaze remains steady, and there's no hint of

emotion on his face. I wonder if he's in shock. It's not unusual for a client to be in denial about their grief.

"It happened when I was a child."

The words shock me to the core. I know what it's like to lose a parent when you're young. This guy's been through hell.

"How old were you?"

"Six."

My heart goes out to this silent stranger. No six-year-old should lose their mother.

"I'm so sorry."

He keeps staring at me. I don't look away.

As much as I'm drawn to this man, I have to set that aside and be professional. It doesn't matter that his presence in the room is making my body do all sorts of weird things. I have to treat him with the care and dignity he deserves.

"That must have been heartbreaking for a six-year-old."

Sting keeps looking at me. In his eyes, I see a flash of pain, the first sign that I've gotten through to him.

His brow furrows, and he breathes deeply through his nose. My heart breaks to see his pain, but it can be an essential part of healing.

"Do you want to talk to me about what happened?"

He takes a few more deep breaths and finally looks away, breaking eye contact.

I let out a breath I didn't know I was holding. It feels like a breakthrough.

"My mother was a junkie."

I keep my expression neutral even as my heart breaks. No little boy deserves the heartbreak that addiction brings.

Sting puts his elbows on his knees and leans forward, resting his head in his hands.

"She wasn't a bad person. It was hard for her raising me on her own."

I let him talk while I listen, taking in his pain, holding it, hopefully lessening it.

"I don't know when she started. It was something I always knew. Mom slumped on the couch. Mom blurry-eyed and stumbling, spilling the milk as she got me breakfast. I learned how to look after myself."

I envision Sting as a little boy, afraid and alone and having to do things himself that no boy should. I long to reach across the coffee table and take his hand. But I refrain, keeping it professional even as my heart breaks for him.

"There were always needles in the house. She would shoot up in front of me, not caring anymore if I saw. I would hold her hair back when she was sick and wipe the sweat off her forehead with a damp cloth. Then one day, she had a bad reaction. She started shaking and puking…"

He holds his head, the emotion making it too hard to go on.

Instinctively I lean toward him, until I'm close enough to smell the perspiration beading on his skin.

"I called an ambulance, and I held her until they came. But it was too late. She died in my arms."

My chest tightens, and my hand goes to my throat. Memories of my father lying in pools of blood while I looked on flood my brain.

"Do you know what it's like to watch a parent die?"

He asks it rhetorically, but he has no idea that I do. Like him, I watched my father's bleeding body as the life ebbed away from him.

I know the horror, the helplessness. The feeling that the one person in the world who could provide for you was gone.

"I do."

My hand is on Sting's shoulder before I realize I'm out of

my seat. Sting looks up and his eyes are dewy, such a big, strong man made vulnerable by this pain he's been carrying around all these years.

Our eyes meet, and this time the connection feels equal. His look is softer, searching, vulnerable.

"You must have felt scared."

My voice comes out in a whisper as I recall the night twelve years ago, the fear that gripped my heart.

"I was frightened, and I felt alone."

"Yes." He's describing all the things I felt. The memories of that night are coming back. The gunshot, the blood, the terror.

My arm touches his shoulders, needing to comfort him, needing to solidify this connection. It's unprofessional. You're not meant to touch the clients. But to hell with that. I already know Sting is never going to be a regular client.

"I was scared there was no one to look after me."

My hand circles his back just above the shoulder blade, sending sparks of heat down my arm.

"I've had to look after myself ever since."

He turns his head and his face is only inches from mine. I smell sweet coffee on his breath along with a musky, masculine scent.

His pale eyes are wide and vulnerable, and I know exactly how he feels. I spent the rest of my life being independent, looking after myself and my mom who was torn open by grief.

He gets me. This man understands what I went through, and I see his pain.

His fingertips brush my cheek, and I know without regret that I'm about to cross a line.

I lean forward and press my lips to his.

Sting's lips part for me, like he's been expecting it. He

kisses me back, hard and insistent. His hand snakes into my hair, and he jerks my head toward him, pressing my mouth hard against his.

It feels like a sweet release, like something forbidden. His stubble brushes against my cheek as he moves his mouth down my throat and over my neck.

"Liberty…"

My name murmured against my skin sends heat waves coursing through my body. I should stop. I should pull away. But it feels too damn good, too right.

"We shouldn't do this." I attempt a feeble protest. Sting pulls away, and I miss his mouth on my neck.

"You want me to stop?"

His finger trails over my lips and down my neck, making me shiver all the way to my throbbing core.

"No." I shake my head imperceptibly.

Sting stands up and pulls me to my feet.

His hand wraps around my throat, and for an instant I can't breathe. His eyes blaze as he squeezes my neck. I stumble backward, halfway between terrified and turned on, until my back hits the wall.

My eyes must be wide because Sting eases off my throat.

"You want me to keep going?"

As he says it, his other hand slides between my legs. I'm embarrassed by how damp it is there.

"Yes," I whimper.

My eyes dart to the door. If anyone came in now, I'd lose my job. I'd lose my license. I'd lose everything. But the feel of his hands on my throat, his fingers between my legs, his breath on my face—it's all too much. I want him. I don't care about the rest.

"You worried someone might hear us?"

There's a wolfish look on his face that should signal danger but makes my nipples pebble with need.

"Don't worry. I'll make sure you come quietly."
I am so fucked.

9
STING

My groin rubs against Liberty, feeling her damp pussy through her flimsy leggings. There's only a square of fabric that separates her sweet cunt from me, and I can smell her arousal.

I keep one hand on her delicate throat, squeezing her neck gently. With the other hand, I slide into her leggings and down the fabric of her panties until I feel her rough bush on my fingertips.

She moans as I find her sweet spot. She's dripping wet. I run my hand between her pussy lips, coating my fingers.

My hand moves down her throat to her breasts, pulling her top aside to get into her bra. Her nipples are peaked nubs, and I rub one with my thumb while stroking her down below.

I'm a fucking animal. I know I am for pushing this sweet angel against the wall.

But I got too vulnerable. I started to feel something soft, something warm inside that I closed off long ago.

I don't want to be that vulnerable, so I make up for it

now, biting Liberty's nipple and squeezing her throat as I draw her to a messy climax.

I don't speak. I've done enough talking today. I retreat into silence, listening to Liberty moan and breathing in her musky scent.

My fingers slide into her tight cunt, the wet walls sucking me in.

This is what heaven feels like. Right here. An angel writhing in ecstasy on the end of your fingers.

I let her ride my hand, watching the way her neck tilts backward, her eyes rolling into her head, her brow creasing as she explodes on my palm.

My mouth covers hers to stifle her noises, noises that I know will be etched into my memory for eternity.

When she stops trembling, I slide my fingers out of her and bring them to my nose, breathing in her heady scent. Now I know what Liberty smells like.

My hand releases its grip on her, and her head rolls forward. Her eyes are soft and dreamy. She's the vulnerable one now.

"I wasn't expecting that."

Neither the fuck was I.

I don't know what to say. I want to tell her she's mine, that I'll take care of her and make up for all the hurt I caused. But I don't know how to say the words. I can't be the guy who whispers sweet nothings in her ear.

I hand Liberty a box of tissues and turn away while she cleans herself up.

When I look back, she's looking at me expectantly. This is my chance, my chance with an angel. But I don't know what she needs.

"I want to take you to dinner." It comes out gruffer than I mean it to.

She gives me a wry smile. "You're supposed to take a woman out before you ravish her."

I'm so relieved to see her smile that I feel my mouth tipping up at the corners. It takes me a moment to realize I'm smiling too. It's not something I do often.

"Come by my place and I'll cook for you."

That's an invitation I'm not going to turn down.

"Tonight."

She frowns. "I'm seeing my mom tonight. Make it tomorrow."

I nod but don't say anything. There's nothing to say.

Liberty's giving me a chance, a chance that I don't deserve. Her radiance emanates from her like a fucking angel. It's so bright I can't look away. Her brightness exposes all my dark shadows, and I feel unworthy next to her.

I make myself smile like an ordinary guy would. I even plant a chaste kiss on her cheek, even though I'm aching to tip her head back, push her to her knees, and shove my cock in her mouth.

I need to swallow that dark side of me. I need to walk toward the light, to pretend to be a man worthy of an angel.

"See you tomorrow," I say casually, even though I hate speaking more than necessary. For Liberty, I'll find my voice. For Liberty, I'd tip the fucking world on its head.

As I shut the door behind me, I bring my fingers to my mouth and suck her sticky sweetness off them.

I can pretend to be a normal guy, but deep down I'm a fucking animal.

10
LIBERTY

Two days later, my stomach is in knots as I stir the pot of bubbling bolognaise and wait for Sting to arrive.

I'm not sure what it is about this man that's got me so worked up. When I think back to the other day in the office, my knees tremble and my core throbs.

I could have gotten fired for what I did with a client. It was brazen and risky and oh so good.

A hot blush creeps up my neck as I remember the feel of his hands on me and how my body responded.

As soon as Sting left my office, I emailed Katie, one of the other counselors, and transferred him to her.

I can't work with someone I'm involved with. And whatever happens tonight, I'm already involved.

The doorbell rings. I smooth my skirt and check my hair in the entryway mirror before opening the door.

Sting takes up the whole door frame with his large build. He's holding a single red rose, and he holds it out to me.

"Thank you."

Our fingers brush as I take the rose, and I feel a jolt of

electricity. There's no denying the chemistry between us. I've never felt anything like it before.

It may have been a stupid risk I took in my office. It may have been a forward thing to do with a practical stranger. But I've learned that life is short. You need to grab those experiences when you can. As the warmth from his touch spreads through my body, I don't regret a thing.

Sting follows me to the kitchen, and I find a vase for the rose.

"Did you get a call from your new therapist?"

Sting looks confused.

"I can't see you anymore if we're going to…" I trail off, not sure how to finish my sentence and suddenly feeling shy.

Sting cocks his head. "What exactly are we doing, Liberty?"

As he says it, he takes my wrist. My pulse jumps up a notch under his touch.

"After what happened, I can't be your therapist."

He pulls me toward him until my skirt brushes against his jeans. "I don't need you to be my therapist."

His pale blue eyes search mine, and I think he's going to kiss me. But he lets go.

"Dinner smells good."

I turn away to hide the rush of disappointment. One touch from Sting and my body aches to feel his hands on me. From the bulge in his trousers, I know he feels the same.

I guess I should feel good that he wants conversation before giving in to what we both know is going to happen here tonight. That means it's more than just physical for him.

"I hope you like bolognaise."

I give the sauce a final stir, then dish up the meal.

My apartment is small, but with Sting around, it feels tiny.

I pull the table out from the wall at the end of the kitchen, and he squeezes his bulky frame into the wooden chair.

The single rose sits in a glass between us, candlelight casting the petals into dark shadows.

"Did you grow up around here?" I ask between mouthfuls.

"I was passed around foster care after my mom died."

Of course he was. I shouldn't have brought up his childhood. That's for his new therapist to deal with.

"How about you?"

Sting seems happier to not be talking about himself, so I don't push it.

"I grew up in Cod Cove."

It's a rich seaside resort up the coast. Most people are surprised when they hear that's where I'm from, but if he's surprised, Sting doesn't show it.

"I moved here with my mom after my father died."

Sting stops chewing and sets his fork down. His hand closes over mine.

"I'm sorry about that."

His look is genuine, and he seems so sincere. It breaks something open in me.

As we eat our dinner, I tell him about the night my father was killed, about how I heard a struggle and hid under the bed in my parents' room.

How the fight came into the room and two men dropped to the floor. The gunshot that made my ears ring, then the blood. Dad's blood that splattered over the floor and onto my face.

How the man looked at me, his face shadowed and grim, and I was sure I was going to die. But he spared my life.

How I kept hidden under the bed until Mom came home.

I don't tell him it was her screams that spurred me to

action, that I calmly called the ambulance, even though it was hours too late.

That I made my mother some soothing tea and wrapped her in a blanket to ease the shock. That when the police took my statement, I didn't cry once. That it was only hours later after I had put Mom to bed and went to brush my teeth that I realized I had blood on my face.

By the time I'm finished telling my story, we've finished eating and Sting is holding my hand across the table.

His thumb rubs my skin soothingly. His expression is all concern.

I look down. He came to me as a patient dealing with a grief he's been holding on to for a long time and now I'm burdening him with my old trauma that I've long since dealt with.

"I'm sorry."

He says it with such intensity, as if he's the one responsible. His concern is touching, and I get it. He's saying he wants to take my hurt away.

"It was a long time ago."

I stand up and take the plates to the sink.

"Is that why you became a grief counselor?"

If only he knew. But I'm not ready to be completely honest with him.

"Yeah," I say because it's easier than explaining the truth. It's what most people believe, that the experience I went through made me want to help others through their grief.

"Do you like chocolate mousse?"

I'm done talking about the past, and Sting takes the hint.

"I've never had it."

My shocked face makes him chuckle. Then I remember how deprived his childhood was, and my heart squeezes for him.

"Then tonight's your lucky night."

I pull the mousse out of the fridge. It's my mom's recipe and I splurged on the fancy ingredients to make it perfect. Now I'm glad that I did.

If Sting's never had a homemade dessert, I'll be the one to give him all the sweet things he's missed out on.

I put some mousse on a plate and bring it over to the table.

"Close your eyes and open your mouth."

He gives me a wary look but does as he's told. I put a bit of mousse on a spoon and slide it between his lips.

His mouth closes around the spoon, and I slide it out of his mouth, watching his expression as the mousse dissolves on his tongue.

"Mmmm." His expression softens. "That's good."

His eyes flutter open, and he reaches for the bowl and spoon.

"Now it's your turn."

Sting's gaze flickers to my lips. A flash of heat zings through my core. He takes a spoonful of mousse and indicates for me to sit.

I do as I'm told and close my eyes, letting my mouth drop open.

The sweet, velvety chocolate slides onto my tongue, and I can't help the moan that escapes my lips. That is the best mousse. With my eyes closed, the flavors are accentuated, exploding on my taste buds.

The spoon taps at my lips, and I open my mouth, letting Sting feed me another mouthful. It's gone too soon and I want more.

"More."

Cold metal on my cheek sends a quiver down my spine as Sting runs the spoon down my jaw and over my throat.

"You want more?" His voice is raspy, sending a zing of heat through my body.

I'm not sure what this new game is, but I'm here to play.

"More please."

I hear the scrape of the spoon against the bowl and a moment later I feel it on my lips. As I part my lips, instead of sliding into my mouth, the spoon darts away out of reach.

"Hey."

My eyes flicker open. Sting's standing above me, his eyes hooded with desire. He slides the spoon into my mouth, and his eyes never leave mine as I suck the sweet stuff off of it.

His hand cups my jaw. He leans forward, kissing me softly.

My body disintegrates into him, and I feel as melty as the mousse I just swallowed.

11
STING

As Liberty's lips close around the spoon, my dick lengthens. I need those lips on me. Now.

My mouth presses against hers, and I taste the chocolate on her tongue.

The encounter in the office was rough and urgent, too needy. Tonight, I want to take it slow. I want to show Liberty I'm not an animal.

She's vulnerable after telling me about her father, and I want to wrap her up and protect her, to let her know that she's safe with me.

Yeah, I know how hypocritical that sounds since I'm the one that killed him. But what's done is done. All I can do now is be a better man, the man Liberty needs me to be.

My hand slides around the back of her head, and I gently guide her upwards until she's on her feet.

Her body presses against mine, and I groan as my dick pushes against my pants. I want to push her against the wall and rub myself all over her. But I resist. This has to be slow and sweet, everything she needs.

My hands slide down her throat and over her breasts to

wrap around her waist. I pull her toward me as my kisses travel over her soft skin.

"Where's the bedroom?"

I could take her on the kitchen table, but I won't. Not tonight. Tonight, she needs to believe that I'm a good man, that I deserve her.

"Follow me."

Liberty throws a saucy look over her shoulder as she takes my hand. I let her lead me through the small living room and to the bedroom at the back of the apartment. It's right next to the bathroom, and I've already seen through her shear curtains to what's in here.

She leads me to the bed, and we stand facing each other. My hands grasp at her top, pulling it off. I have to force myself to go slow, even as her nipples peak enticingly.

I take my time peeling off each layer, and when I'm done, I let her peel off mine.

When she slides off my t-shirt, there's a gasp.

"What happened?"

She trails her fingers over the scar that runs from the top of my shoulder to halfway down my chest. Her fingers are light on the puckered skin. So soft. The tenderness almost undoes me.

"I got it in Iraq."

It's a lie, but I'm not going to get into what happened in my first foster home. The bullying from the older kids. The fire and the burning wood they held on my skin. I've taken too much of Liberty's sympathy.

"I didn't know you were in the Army."

I kiss her then, silencing her questions. I don't like to talk, especially not about my past. That outburst in her counseling room is about as much as I'm willing to share. Maybe one day she'll hear the rest of it but not tonight.

Her skin tastes like traces of chocolate and Italian herbs.

She must have spent the whole day in the kitchen and that touches me, the effort she's gone to for me.

My kisses become more urgent as I run my hands, my mouth, and my tongue over her body. At some point, I push her gently back on to the bed.

Our lovemaking becomes a blur. I throw Liberty's legs over my shoulders and slowly taste her sweet pussy, licking and nibbling and finger fucking her until her moans turn to screams of pleasure.

When she's finished coming, I nestle between her thighs.

I long to turn her over, to take her roughly from behind, to pound all my emptiness into her. But not tonight.

Tonight, I must be the better man she thinks I am.

I grab a condom from my pocket, even though I long to breed her. I can be patient. Tonight, I'm the good guy, the thoughtful guy.

She helps me slide the condom on, and the feeling of her hands around my cock is almost enough to send me over the edge.

She shuffles to the side of the bed. Still standing, I line myself up with her entrance. Her eyes widen as I push into her just a few inches at a time, giving her time to adjust.

My hands grab her hips, and I lift her up as I slam in the rest of the way. Liberty cries out and her hips buck. I'm right there to meet her, and we thrust together.

Panting and sweating, our bodies move as one. Her legs wrap around my back, her heels digging into me.

Watching her orgasm builds makes my balls pull up tight. At the same time that she explodes, I release. We come together, screaming out our pleasure as our bodies convulse. It's like nothing I've experienced before, this joining. The emptiness explodes out of me, and for one beautiful moment I feel like there's somewhere I belong.

. . .

Afterward, Liberty runs a bath, performing the rituals I've watched her do through the window. The bubble bath, the oils, and the candles.

We slip into the bath together, and she leans her back against me. Through the window I see the darkness of the apartment building opposite.

The candlelight flickers against her skin, making it look golden.

"Some people put a candle in the window for those that have gone," I say as I nuzzle against her neck. "They believe that the light will guide them back, that the people you love will come back to you."

Liberty leans her head back on my chest. "I've got the one I love right here."

She sighs deeply and her body goes heavy. After a few moments, I'm sure she's fallen asleep.

It's peaceful. I let my mind drift. How easy it is to pretend to be a better man, to fit into Liberty's life like I belong, like I deserve an angel like Liberty.

What if I could always be this man? What if I could have this every night, a soft woman to love and a warm body next to me to hold?

What if I could be a better man?

12

LIBERTY

Three weeks later...

There's a strange sound coming from the kitchen. I dress quickly and follow the noise of clinking dishes. Sting has his hands in the sink, a dish cloth thrown over his shoulder, and he's whistling to himself as he cleans up the plates from the previous night.

I've never heard Sting whistle. The sound lends a cheerful note to the morning. He's come a long way from the broken man I met in my counseling session a few weeks ago.

"Good morning."

My hands slide around his waist, and he turns to give me a lingering kiss. His soapy hand brushes my cheek, leaving wet suds on my chin. I bat him away playfully but not before I notice the grazes on his knuckles.

"What happened?" I capture his hand and examine the raw marks on his skin. They look fresh. I could have sworn they weren't there yesterday.

"Just a work injury." He pulls his hands away from mine.

"I didn't notice them last night."

He gives me a wicked grin and slides his hand between my legs.

"That's because you were too distracted by my face buried between your thighs."

The memory of last night makes my pussy clench. We started in the bath and finished panting together in the bedroom. It's true. He might have had those scars when he came home and I never noticed.

I don't mention that I woke in the night and Sting's side of the bed was empty.

The first time it happened, I got out of bed looking for him, anxiety clawing at my stomach when he wasn't in the apartment. I waited in the living room until he slipped in the door a few hours later.

He told me he gets insomnia sometimes and slips out to walk the streets until he feels tired again.

Now when I wake and Sting's not there, I go back to sleep. If wandering the street helps him get past his demons, then I won't stand in his way.

Sting goes back to the dishes, and I ignore the gnawing feeling in my stomach.

I must not have noticed the scars yesterday. Sting wouldn't be humming so happily if he was hiding something. Would he?

"I guess the therapy's going well, then?"

I shouldn't ask, but I'm curious about his sessions. I've never run into him at the center, and I won't ask Katie about them. That would be unprofessional.

Sting gives me a confused look.

"Your counseling sessions? You seem a lot happier."

"Yeah." He turns back to the dishes. "They're going good."

I've learned not to expect many words from Sting. That's fine by me. We have other ways to communicate.

I butter him a couple slices of toast, and we eat together

at the small table. There's a splattering of rain at the window, and I look out to the gray skies.

"Can you still work in the rain?"

Sting glances out the window thoughtfully.

"Yeah. The roof's on. I can give you a lift on the way to the site."

I finish getting ready for work, and Sting dons his workman's hat and bright yellow vest. I wonder what my father would think if he were still alive. His little girl hooking up with a construction worker. Daddy would have hated it. The thought makes me smile.

Before we leave, I grab the bag of sandwiches I made last night and hand them to Sting.

"Thank you."

He gives me a tender kiss, and we head out to work together. I hum a tune as we catch the elevator. His good mood is infectious. Sting clasps my hand tightly and keeps hold of it all the way to his car.

My life has been transformed by this man over the last few weeks. My hand in his feels snug and warm and exactly where it's supposed to be.

The rain is light when Sting pulls up outside my work. Before I can open the car door, he reaches over and cups my chin in his hand.

"I love you, Liberty."

It's not the first time he's said it, but my heart still flutters.

"I love you too."

He's smiling as I slide out of the car, and he doesn't leave until I'm safely inside the building. Before I go in the door, I turn and give him a final wave, the smile wide on my face.

Yup, my life has changed in the last few weeks, and I've got that kind gentle giant to thank for it.

13
STING

Liberty waves at me before going into her building. I wave back, the smile on my face genuine. I've gotten so good at pretending to be a nice, normal guy that some days I feel like I'm almost becoming one.

As soon as she disappears inside the building, I gun the engine. I drive around town for a while before stopping in a remote industrial area on the edge of town.

I ditch my hard hat and hi vis vest and change into my dark clothes. The work I've got today needs stealth, not fluorescent safety gear.

It was an easy lie to tell that I work in construction. It's the kind of job she won't ask too many questions about. The kind of job where I can explain away any cuts and scrapes I get from my real work.

Every time I leave Liberty in the middle of the night, it gets harder and harder. The first time she was up waiting for me when I got home, and I fed her a story about walking the streets to help my insomnia. She seems to buy it because she's an honest woman. It hasn't occurred to her that I might be lying.

But better she believes that than the truth. That the scars on my hand are from when I was called in to question one of Damon's business associates about some missing stock.

I got Damon the answer he needed, but I left feeling sick.

It made me sick to think about Liberty at home in bed, convinced that I'm a good guy walking the streets to ease my troubled heart. If she knew the truth, it would break her.

My phone beeps with the details of the hit.

The info we got last night exposed a bad element in Damon's supply chain. Someone got greedy and has been going behind Damon's back. I've been sent to eliminate him.

Like I eliminated Liberty's father twelve years ago.

I shake the thought from my head. There's no place for regret in my line of work.

I drive to the address and park a few blocks away. With my gear in a tote bag, I walk quickly down the street.

The address is a storage facility with a gated entrance and CCTV cameras. There's a back corner that's a blind spot, and I cut a hole in the fence and crawl through.

I prefer to be up high for a hit, so I scale the side of a storage container and make my way over the rooftops until I get near the unit number I've been given.

Keeping low, I crawl over the roofs until I'm looking down on the empty lane in front of me, the yellow storage units in a tight line.

If my intel is correct, it'll be another twenty minutes before he gets here. I pull my rifle out and I wait.

Eventually, a car turns into the row between the storage units and drives slowly down the lane. It's a tan-colored station wagon with a dent in the passenger door. Whoever this guy is, he's not spending his cash on fancy cars.

The car stops and a man gets out. He's got to be around my age with graying hair and the start of a saggy gut.

Before he shuts the car door, I get a glimpse of a child seat in the back and a colorful soft toy. The seat's empty, but the knowledge that he's a family man makes my stomach turn.

He's somebody's father. Somebody's husband. There are people who love him and whose lives will be affected by what I do today.

My finger eases off the trigger, and I wipe the sweat from my brow. Hesitation is dangerous. That's when things go wrong.

This guy knew what he was doing when he got greedy and crossed Damon Fletcher.

But there's a new voice in my head, a softer voice that wonders if maybe this guy was just trying to do what's best for his family, like start a college fund for his kid.

I think about his kid and what will happen to them without a dad. Will the mom be able to raise the kid on her own, to provide for them? Or will she spiral out of control and resort to alcohol or drugs to make her feel better?

My hand strains on the trigger as blood thunders in my ears. I've killed a lot of people in my life and I've never thought twice. Why now?

I know why.

Because three weeks of pretending to be a better guy for Liberty is turning me into a better guy.

The man unlocks a padlock and pulls open a roller door to one of the units. If I'm going to do it, now is the time. Before he goes inside. Now's my chance.

My finger trembles, but I don't pull the trigger.

Maybe I like being a better guy. Maybe the lie I'm living with Liberty doesn't have to be a lie. I could get a job in construction and be the regular guy she thinks I am.

The man goes inside his storage unit, and I lower my rifle.

I don't want this life anymore. Liberty has shown me a different kind of life, a better side of me. I don't have to be an animal. I can choose what I am.

I can be the kind of man who deserves her, and I will be.

14
LIBERTY

J try to concentrate on the man with his head in his hands, but my gaze keeps creeping to the clock on the wall. Ten more minutes of the group session, then I'm done for the day.

Then I can go home to Sting.

My mind goes over the cryptic message I got from him today.

For a man who doesn't talk much, he sure has a way with words.

You've made me a better man.

I'm so glad I found you.

I should be paying attention to the participant in front of me working through his grief, not thinking about Sting. I sit on my hands to stop from fidgeting and focus on the man talking.

My eyes wander to the clock. Five more minutes. Time to wrap the session up.

I wait for the man to finish before offering words of encouragement. One of the regulars pats his arm reassuringly, and they both go over to the refreshment station.

I gather my purse and head for the door.

I'm walking past the reception desk when I meet Katie coming down the corridor. Over the last few weeks, I've refrained from asking her how her sessions with Sting have been going.

But seeing him in such a good mood lately, it's obvious she's doing good work with him.

"Whatever you're doing with Sting, it's working."

She gives me a puzzled look, her eyebrows pulled together. "Who?"

It's not like Katie to forget a client.

"Sting, the big guy. I referred him to you." I don't explain why. I could still get in trouble for how our relationship started.

"Oh, yeah." Katie's face lights up in recognition. "I called, but he never booked an appointment."

My stomach twists in an uneasy knot. She must be thinking about someone else.

"I emailed you about him?"

She furrows her brow. "Yeah, the guy who lost his mom when he was a kid. He never got back to me."

If Sting never made the appointment, then he hasn't been coming to counseling. The uneasy feeling in my stomach creeps up to my chest.

"Are you okay?" Katie asks.

"Yeah." I put on a tight smile. "I must have been mistaken."

I hurry out the door with the uneasy feeling in my gut. Sting hasn't exactly lied, but he hasn't been honest either.

He could have told me he didn't continue the counseling. It makes me wonder what else he hasn't been honest about.

By the time I walk the few blocks home, the uneasy feeling has mostly gone. It must be a misunderstanding.

I've gone over our conversations from the last few weeks, and I can't be sure if I ever asked him directly about the counseling. Sting doesn't talk much, and I must have assumed he was still going. He just never corrected me.

It's a small thing and not worth worrying about.

I'm feeling better by the time I open the door to my apartment. There's the smell of roast chicken coming from the kitchen, and I go in to find Sting preparing a meal.

Sting doesn't cook. I learned that about him. He was looked after in the Army and never learned to cook properly since.

Instead, he's bought a roast chicken from the supermarket, and he's arranged it on a plate with vegetables and salad.

There's a row of candles alight on the table and an open bottle of wine. Handel's "Messiah" plays softly in the background. My mom used to take me to hear the orchestra play, and I've always loved classical music.

"What's all this for?"

I slide my arms around Sting's waist, and he gives me a slow kiss on the lips.

"I wanted to surprise you."

I'm touched that he's gone to this much effort for me. He's even got a tablecloth and napkins on the table so it looks like a restaurant.

"It's lovely. What's the occasion?"

I mean it jokingly, but Sting has a serious look about him.

"Wait here."

He ducks into the living room and comes back with a bunch of red roses. There must be twelve in the bouquet, each one a perfect blood red.

He hands them over solemnly, and as I take them, I notice a small box attached to the bouquet. It's a velvet box, just the right size for a ring.

My heart skips a beat. "What's this?"

Sting sinks to one knee in front of me. My heart flutters at what I know is coming next.

"Liberty, since you came into my life, you've taught me how to be a better man. I want to spend the rest of my life with you. Will you marry me?"

His words fill my heart and any last doubt melts away. It's been only a few weeks, but I feel it as intensely as he does. Sting flips open the small box and takes the ring out.

I stifle a gasp.

It's beautiful. A shiny gold band with a large round diamond in the center, encrusted with smaller stones around the edge. It's pure gold, like the jewelry my mom used to own, and the diamonds are real too. I can tell by the way they sparkle in the candlelight.

He looks up at me, his eyes imploring. This is crazy, but it's right. For the first time in twelve years, I feel anchored. I feel safe, protected, like someone will always look out for me.

"Yes." Sting visibly relaxes, and I realize he was unsure of my answer. "Yes, yes, yes."

I cast the roses aside, and he slips the ring on my finger. It sparkles in the candlelight.

I throw myself at Sting, and he embraces me in a tight hug.

It may be crazy fast but it feels so right.

As he showers kisses over my face and lips, I push down the nagging voice inside that wonders how the hell a construction worker can afford a ring that size.

15
STING

"You can't just quit. It doesn't work like that."

I stare straight ahead at a spot over Damon's head as I wait for him to process that I don't work for him anymore.

"You're not the first person who's tried to walk away from this job. It's not a normal job, Sting. You don't just hand in a resignation letter."

I knew Damon wouldn't take it well. I've been his man for a long time, the one who gets his hands dirty with the deeds he doesn't want to do. The one who until a few weeks ago was too dead inside to believe he was good for anything else.

Damon will have to find another soulless foot soldier. I'm done.

I knew it the moment I couldn't carry out the hit. I don't want to be that person anymore, delivering a silent, quick death to someone else's enemies.

Damon can do his dirty work himself.

He was furious I didn't make the hit the other day, but it bought the target some time to make it right. He offered

Damon a cut of his new business venture. They're back on good terms. Business partners again.

If I'd gone through with the hit, Damon would have lost some business and a family would have lost their father.

Damon's gotten less rational as he ages, greedier and less tolerant of those who go against him. It's the right time to get out.

I've got my future with Liberty now. I've got enough money stashed away to keep us comfortable for years. But I'll look for a job, something straight, something where she can be proud of me.

"What's brought this on?" Damon asks. "Why the change of heart all of a sudden?"

I won't tell him about Liberty. I have no doubt he'll find it out for himself.

"I grew a heart."

Damon chuckles a soft laugh. "Found some pussy more like it."

I jump the desk and have my hands around his throat before I know what I'm doing. My blood thunders in my ears. My vision tinges red.

"Say that again and I'll kill you."

The door bursts open, and Damon's men rush in with their guns raised. I loosen my grip and put my hands in the air. I didn't come here to kill anyone or get killed today.

Damon's seething. He looks at me with pure contempt.

"That was a bad move, Sting. But what can I expect from an animal I pulled off the streets?"

My fists clench. I'm aching to tear the man apart.

He's right. I was an animal when he found me, and I've behaved like one ever since because that's what he needed me to be. That's all he ever saw me as.

Liberty sees me as something else. With her I'm something better.

I won't debase myself today by playing into the role he wants me to.

"I'm done."

I turn around with my hands in the air. The guards eye me warily as I take a step toward the door.

They're big guys but not as big as me. I can see the fear on their faces. If I make a move, I'll take at least one of them out before they can shoot me.

"Let him go," Damon mutters from behind me. "I'll release this animal back into the wild."

I don't look back as I step out of Damon's office for the last time.

When I get home that evening, I take Liberty roughly, bent over the kitchen table, pumping my soul into her. She moans and cries out, but I can't be gentle. Not today. She senses my need and she lets me have it, arching her back as I slam into her, my hands grabbing her hips so hard there will be bruises tomorrow.

My anger spurts out with my cum, coating her insides. No condom today, just me giving all of myself to her. As I release into Liberty, I feel my tension ease away. She's my safe space, the light I cling onto.

I pull her tight to me and press my thundering heart next to hers. Her soft hands caress my cheek as she makes soothing noises. She doesn't know what's got me so riled up, but she knows how to calm me, with gentle strokes and soothing noises. The same way a keeper pacifies a wild animal.

16
LIBERTY

I play with the ring nervously, spinning it around my finger as I ring the doorbell of the Fletchers' house. It takes a few moments before the butler opens the door.

"Miss Jones. This way please."

I'm ushered into a sitting room with a large mahogany desk in one corner. It's where Damon works when he's at home, and the fact I've been shown in here tells me this isn't a social call.

Damon's assistant called me two days ago and said Damon wanted to see me. There was no information as to what it was about. I assume it's to do with the funding for the center. I hope like hell he's not going to cut it.

The butler comes back with a tray of refreshments, and I pour myself a cup of coffee. It's another few minutes before Damon enters the room.

"Liberty." He gives me an indulgent smile and a fatherly hug. "Good of you to come."

He says it as if I had a choice, but we both know if Damon Fletcher summons you, you don't refuse.

He asks politely about my mother, and we exchange pleasantries for a few moments. The whole time I'm wondering when he'll get to the point.

I have to sit on my hands to stop fidgeting, and my stomach's in knots thinking about what it will mean for the center without his generous donations.

"You must be wondering why I asked you here."

"Are you cutting funding for the center?" I blurt out.

Damon looks surprised.

"No. Not at all. The work you're doing at the center is vital for this community."

I let out a deep breath I didn't know I was holding and sink into the plush couch, the knot in my stomach unfurling.

Damon must sense my relief because he puts a reassuring hand on my shoulder.

"I'll keep funding the center as long as you need it. You can be assured of that."

Relief flows through me. The center is safe. The people who need help will still be able to access it.

The relief is short lived. If this isn't about the center, then why has he brought me here?

Damon walks around the back of the mahogany desk and picks up a file.

"I hate to reopen old wounds, but some new information has come to light about your father's death."

I sit up straight on the sofa, my chest tightening. This is not at all what I was expecting.

After my father's death, I was occupied with helping my mom, making sure she could get back on her feet.

It was only when I was older that I asked Damon about my father, and even then I only asked once. They were business partners. Damon claimed his enemies brought my father down. He was tight lipped and refused to discuss it further.

As the years went on, I resigned myself to the fact that I would never know the reason why he died and that his killer would walk free.

Damon's look has turned serious. He takes a seat on a low chair opposite me, holding the folder in his hands. It's a flimsy cardboard file, but the way he holds it makes it seem weighty.

I reach out my hand, but he hesitates in handing it over.

"There are things in here that you may not like."

The warning makes my stomach clench. My father wasn't a saint. I know that better than anyone. It's been twelve years since he passed. I'm suddenly not so sure I want to know the truth about him.

My hand falters, but before I can pull away, Damon shoves the file into my palm, and I clasp it in my hand.

"It's always better to know the truth, Liberty. It can hurt, but it will set you free."

Damon's watching me carefully, and I can't read his expression. With trembling hands, I open the folder.

I'm not expecting to see a photo of Sting peering out at me. There are less lines on his face, and his hair is a dark brown, with no flecks of silver. Yet there's no mistaking it's him.

I glance up at Damon, confusion written all over my face.

"This is the man who killed your father."

The words sit in the air, suspended for a moment like sharp knives waiting to fall. My heart seems to stop, suspended in this moment of time between ignorance and knowledge. And when it beats again, the knives fall, piercing my chest and stabbing my heart until I can't breathe.

Gasping for air, I double over. The room goes blurry. I can hear Damon's voice but it seems far away.

I'm aware of the butler running in and someone propping me up and pressing a glass of whiskey to my lips.

The strong draught revives me and I cough, pulling big puffs of air into my lungs.

My mind spins. He can't mean Sting. It can't be true.

But I know. I know deep down in a place where it hurts. I know the truth of it.

Memories of that night cloud my brain. The sounds of a struggle. Crawling under the bed. The heavy footsteps. My father falling to the ground with a man on top of him. The animalistic noises they both made as they struggled for the gun. Then the shot and the silence that came after.

The man who turned his head and saw me. His face comes into my vision. His pale eyes. The intense look.

The memory had faded over the years, but now I see Sting, his younger self—the man in the picture. I know it in my bones. That was the face I saw looking back at me that night twelve years ago.

Sting was the man who murdered my father.

I become aware of a voice speaking to me, and I turn to the sound of it.

"Are you all right?"

I focus on Damon's concerned voice. Does he know about my relationship with Sting? He can't know. How could he?

I think back to the last few weeks. Aside from going to work together, we've mostly kept to ourselves, content in our own little world in my apartment.

This has got to be some horrible coincidence.

"I'm sorry. I knew this would be distressing for you. I underestimated the shock."

I take a deep breath, and even though my heart is racing, I make myself put on a calm voice.

"It's just a shock thinking about this all again."

Damon peers at me. "I shouldn't have showed you. I thought you'd want to know." He goes to take the folder, but I pull it away from him.

THE HITMAN'S REDEMPTION

"No. I want to see." There are other papers in the folder, other photos. I don't know what they are, but I need to see it all. I need to understand.

"Stay here as long as you need."

I stand up. I don't want to be here. I want to be at home. On my own.

Sting isn't due home from work for another few hours. I need time to process it all. Maybe there's been a mistake. Maybe Sting wasn't the killer.

But I know in my heart that he is.

I knew something wasn't honest about him. Disappearing in the night, grazes on his knuckles, the unexplained money.

I stand up abruptly.

"Thank you for this, but I'd like to look at it at home."

"Of course. If you're feeling up to it."

Damon is all courtesy and concern, but there's something else in his look that I don't understand. There's triumph behind his concerned expression. I need to get out of here.

"It was just a shock initially. I'm fine." I paint on a smile that doesn't fool Damon, but he doesn't push me.

"I'll have one of my men drive you home."

I know there's no point in arguing, so I accept the lift.

The whole way home the folder sits heavily on my lap. I dare not open it until I'm home because seeing Sting's face again—how he was when he killed my father—might make me lose it.

17
STING

It's almost dark by the time I come out of the meeting with my solicitor. The arrangements have been put in place. If Damon decides to take revenge by eliminating me, all my estate will go to Liberty.

I don't think Damon's that stupid. He'll have a hard time recruiting his next hitman if the last one disappears. I made sure I've got insurance with that too.

I met with Karl, Damon's son-in-law, and told him if I disappear it's on Damon. He may not have any sway with his father-in-law, but his wife does.

Trinity's a feisty thing and a good businesswoman. She's been trying to convince her father to go legit, and knocking off anyone who crosses him is not going to sit well with her.

It's not that I'm afraid to die, but I don't want Liberty to suffer any more grief.

I make a quick stop at my apartment to change into my construction gear. The place is as empty as when moved in. Liberty has no idea I rent the place nine floors up and right across from hers. Eventually, I'll get rid of it. But not yet.

There are lights on at her place. I think of Liberty making

the dinner, humming along to classical music, her hair wisping around her neck as she waits for me to come home. I change quickly and make my way to her place.

As soon as I open the door to her apartment, I know something's wrong. The house is silent, and there's no smell of dinner cooking.

"Liberty?"

My heart jumps into my throat. I banked that Damon wouldn't go after Liberty. It's not his style to hurt women. But would he go that far to get back at me?

I don't bother to pull my boots off as I tear through the empty kitchen to the living room. I find Liberty sitting on the couch in the dark.

Relief floods me. She's alive.

"Thank god."

I rush to her side and take her in my arms, but she recoils. The movement makes me freeze. There's a look of disgust on her face, and I know in an instant she knows what I am. She knows I'm nothing but an animal.

This is his revenge. I know it before she opens her mouth.

"You killed my father."

Her voice is shaky. I want to comfort her but she recoils from my touch.

I stand up and pace the room, my hand running over my stubble. There's no point denying it. There's no lie I can tell that will make this right.

"Damon told you."

She picks up a folder that's on the coffee table and throws it at me. "He gave me this. New information about my father. It names you as his killer."

I barely recognize the photo of myself from twelve years ago, fresh faced before my first paid kill.

"Is it true?"

There's hurt in her eyes and a sliver of hope. She wants

me to deny it. She wants me to be the good man she knows me as, not the animal that I am.

I meet her eyes. I won't be a coward. I won't deny it. I'll look her in the eye and give her the truth. I owe her that.

"Yes."

Liberty crumples. Her whole body goes soft, and her head falls into her hands. My instinct is to comfort her. I crouch in front her and wrap my arms around her.

Liberty pulls away from me.

"Don't touch me."

Her eyes meet mine. They're dry but full of fire. "Did you know I was his daughter? Did you know when you met me?"

I stand again, my body suddenly feeling too large and brutish for this room.

I've lost her. She's found out what I really am. There's no point in anymore lies. It's time to tell her the whole ugly truth about me.

"Yes. I saw you getting off the bus one night. I followed you home, and when I saw your face, I knew you were the little girl I remember from that night."

"The night you killed my father," she spits.

The venom in her voice makes me flinch. I deserve this. I deserve all of it.

"I never meant to hurt you. I've thought about you every day since that night, and when I came across you again, I couldn't let you go."

She looks disgusted, and I don't blame her. I'm not looking for forgiveness. My deeds are too big for that. I just want to tell her the whole truth.

"I don't even know who you are."

"I work for Damon. Or I did. I quit two days ago, which I guess is why he's showing you this now."

Her brow furrows as she connects the dots.

"Are you saying Damon was behind the killing?"

I hate to tell her this. Damon's been like a father to her. This might shatter her all over again, but it's too late to go back now.

"Yes."

Liberty puts her head in her hands.

"I don't know why. It wasn't my job to ask questions. Damon took me off the streets. He took me in, and I worked for him."

When she looks up, the anger is still on her face. "I don't want to hear your sob story, Sting. I get it. You had a shitty upbringing. That doesn't give you the right to play God."

She's right. Nothing justifies the evil I've done. Nothing.

She stands up now, her anger getting the better of her. "You wormed your way into my life. You made me believe you were someone else."

Her fists come at me and she pummels my chest. I back away with my hands in the air, letting her get her anger out on me.

"Do you even work in construction?"

I shake my head.

"My god, Sting. It was a lie. All of it."

She pounds her fists into my chest, and I grab her wrists. "No. Not all of it. I love you, Liberty. The feelings we have aren't a lie. Those are real."

She pulls away from me. I let her go. She's too distraught. I won't hold her against her will.

"Everything you ever said to me was a lie, Sting." She pulls something out of her pocket. It's the ring I gave her only a few nights before.

"Get out of my house."

She throws the ring at my chest, and it hits me right below the heart. I let it bounce off me and fall to the floor.

"Keep it. If you're ever in any trouble, sell it."

"You're the only one bringing trouble into my life, Sting."

The pain on her face cleaves my heart in two, and there's an ache in my chest knowing I've caused that. Again.

"Liberty…" I take a step toward her, and she puts her hands up.

"That day you came in for counseling. Was that all a lie too?"

I meet her gaze. "I followed you there because I wanted to meet you. But everything I told you about my mother… That was the truth."

There's a flicker of relief on her face. It's not enough, but at least it's something. She knows there was some truth in our connection, and that's going to have to do.

She indicates a bag that I didn't notice by the door. "There's your stuff. I want you to go."

There's no point in arguing. Damon's revenge has been effective. He's exposed me as the animal I am. I knew it was stupid to pretend I was anything else.

"I'll go," I tell her so she knows I won't make a fuss. "But if you're ever in trouble, if you need me, I'll be here."

She's too angry to really listen to what I'm saying. And I don't blame her.

I grab my stuff and leave. As the door clicks behind me, I feel my heart close over. I had a chance, a chance to be something better than I was. But Damon's right. Once an animal, always an animal.

18

LIBERTY

The bed feels cold when I awake with the house empty. Rain splatters against the windows, and I wrap the duvet around me, burrowing under the covers.

There's a dull ache in my chest and an emptiness in my heart. It's been two days since I found out the truth about Sting. Two days since he left.

I hate it that I miss him so much, but the truth is, I do.

I slide out of bed and pad through the empty apartment. It's quiet without him. The only noise is the rain hitting the windowpanes. There's no humming from the kitchen, no clinking of dishes, no smell of his body wash lingering in the air.

I make myself some instant coffee and cradle it in my hands, perching on the edge of the couch. For the last few days, I've been able to keep myself busy with work, but today is Saturday, and I feel the emptiness of the day stretching before me.

On the coffee table is the green file, sitting where I left it.

I haven't wanted to touch it. It felt too raw. But today I slide the file over and flip open the cover.

Sting's photo peers out at me. I turn it over quickly and slide it under the file.

That's not what I want to look at today. There are other papers in the file, but I didn't get further than Sting's image.

Damon told me there were truths in here about my father, things I wasn't going to like. But I doubt anything could be as shocking as finding out your fiancé killed your father.

The first item is a packing receipt. It's faded from use, the ink running and unreadable. It looks like a container that was coming through the port.

I've got no idea what the significance is. I put it aside.

The next paper is a printout of an email exchange. I recognize my father's name in one of the email addresses.

It's talking about a shipment that was coming in. But the details seem sketchy. It makes about as much sense as the shipping docket.

I flip to the next item in the folder, and my breath hitches. It's a series of images. They're black and white and blurry with a time stamp running along the bottom. Freeze frames from a security camera.

There's an open shipping container. There are people inside of it. I hold the blurry images up to the light, squinting to see the detail. Not just people. Women. They're all women. Long hair hanging straggly down their backs. Some sitting, some standing, and one sprawled on the ground, her limbs contorted in a weird shape.

But there's a detail that makes my blood run cold. Every single woman in the photo has her hands behind her back and her shoulders pulled back as if they're bound.

My hands are trembling as I look through the rest of the photos. There are more images. Some show women being ushered off the container into the back of trucks like cattle. Other photos show their bound hands.

There's one woman with a wide-eyed look of terror, but what's more frightening are the resigned expressions that most of the women wear.

There's no doubt in my mind what's happening here. These women are being trafficked.

Mom answers the door on the second knock, looking surprised to see me. Her hair is ruffled, and she pats the side of her head, trying to put it back in place.

"I would have washed my hair if I knew you were coming."

I ignore the chiding tone. I don't give a damn about how she looks. I need answers.

"Damon gave me this."

I hold up the file and Mom peers at it curiously, but I don't miss the look of apprehension that flashes across her face.

"What is it, darling?" Mom puts on a smile, but the way she's fiddling with her rings gives away her nervousness.

"Information about Dad."

The smile falls off Mom's face.

"Have you looked at it?" she asks breathlessly.

"Yes."

Her eyes meet mine. There's no surprise there, just concern, and in that instant, I know she knows.

"You better come in. I'll make you some coffee."

She heads down the hall into the kitchen. As I follow, a surge of anger races through me.

How can she be so calm? How could she have known about this?

"I don't want coffee, Mom. I want to know what the hell this is all about."

I fling the folder at her, and she catches it, holding it aloft as if she's scared of what's inside. She should be.

"Did you know he was trafficking women?"

Mom shakes her head. "No. Of course not. I found out after he was killed."

I don't know if she knows Damon was the one who ordered the hit. I removed the photo of Sting from the folder. Who killed my father has become less relevant in light of what it appears he was up to.

Mom sets the file down on the table in front of her and flicks through the papers. When she gets to the images, she pauses. Her hands tremble as she looks through them.

"Your father wasn't a good man, Liberty."

"I know, Mom. I know he wasn't. The way he treated you, the things he did to me…"

She looks up sharply. I haven't shared everything with my mom. She was so grief-stricken after my father died that I felt I couldn't tell her.

"What did he do?" Her tone is sharp, still the protective mother even though I'm an adult now.

"It's not as bad as you think," I add hastily. "He hit me a few times."

Mom goes still, and I feel the anger bubbling inside her. "He hit you?"

"It's okay, Mom. It doesn't matter now." I hate to see her distressed over something that happened so long ago.

Mom pushes her chair away, and it scrapes along the floor.

"I couldn't protect you." She paces the kitchen, wringing her hands.

Her despair pulls at my heart, and I'm transported back to my childhood. Muffled sounds from my parents' room. Mom's pleading voice and the sharp crack of the blow. The gasps from Mom and the silence as she held in her pain.

"You were protecting yourself," I say.

We never talked about the bruises on Mom's arms, or the way she winced sometimes as she walked. She became known for wearing long, floaty fabrics even in summer that covered her body and hid the bruises.

I hated my father for it, for what he did to her. And as I got older, he turned on me when mom wasn't around to take the blows.

It started with slaps on the backside. Then he would punch me in the stomach, just enough to wind me without leaving any bruises.

It only happened a few times, but it was enough that on the night he was killed, I felt relief.

As I watched the blood trickle down his neck and onto the carpet, I felt a sense of freedom. I felt excited. I felt happy that Mom would no longer suffer.

I had to hide those feelings, bury them inside and pretend I was grieving. But the truth is, I never shed a single tear for my father.

I began to wonder if something was wrong with me. I couldn't understand why Mom was so upset considering the hell he'd put her through. I wondered why I wasn't.

I became fascinated with grief. I read about the different stages so I could pretend I was going through each of them. I sought out others who had lost a loved one and became fascinated with the tears they shed, the raw emotion they experienced. I inhaled other people's grief and listened to their stories so I could better act out the emotions that I was supposed to be experiencing.

That's how I got into counseling. I was drawn to those that were suffering, waiting to feel something, hoping that one day through their grief I might unlock my own.

But, twelve years later, when I think of my father being killed, I still feel relief.

"But why were you so sad when he died?" I could never figure out why Mom grieved for him.

We're facing each other now, our arms entwined, baring our souls in a way we never have before.

"The day your father was killed, I found out what he really was. I wasn't grieving your father. I was grieving those poor women he trafficked."

My head spins. All this time I couldn't understand why Mom was so sad for the man that had abused her. I felt guilty for my lack of grief, but she wasn't grieving him at all.

"When Damon found out your father was using his port to run women through, he was furious. Damon may not have a clean conscience but he would never traffic people."

Mom pauses, and I wonder if she knows it was Damon who ordered the hit on my father. She doesn't mention it, but she must know.

"The day your father died, Damon told me what he had been up to. That hit me more than anything. To know the man you're sleeping next to every night is trafficking women. To realize your home, your wealth, everything you have has been built on the backs of others."

Mom trails off, and something else clicks into place.

"That's why you gave it all away. That's why you sold the house and jewelry."

I always wondered why we went from wealthy to barely making end's meet. I assumed my father hadn't provided for us in his will.

"I couldn't live off his money. I felt physically sick looking at the things we owned knowing where some of that money came from. I gave it away. All of it. To trafficking charities. I didn't want a thing from your father. I didn't want any of it."

There's bitterness in Mom's voice, and I see how hard it must have been for her to realize what her life had been built on. The guilt she must have felt.

"You didn't know."

She shakes her head slowly. "No. I wasn't paying enough attention. I should have known something wasn't adding up."

"Don't beat yourself up, Mom."

The corner of her eyes are wet, and I know there'll always be a sadness there. She'll always carry the guilt of my father. It makes me hate him a little bit more.

"Whoever killed your father did the world a service that day. Women's lives have been better because he's not in the world to ruin them."

Her words shock me, spoken with a quiet conviction. I have no doubt my father was a bad man, but does anyone deserve to die? My mother thinks so, and Damon thought so. Perhaps by Sting doing something bad, it was really a good deed?

"You really think so?"

Mom's hand cups my cheek, her skin rough and crinkled with age, but still a tender mother's touch. "I know so."

Her tears flow over, and I feel my own eyes well up. I always felt guilty about not feeling sad about my father. I had no idea Mom felt the same way.

A sense of freedom overtakes me, coupled with sadness for those women who my dad trafficked.

As tears run down my face, my mom embraces me.

For the first time in twelve years, I'm crying for my father, but it's not for him. It's for the women whose lives he ruined. It's for my brave mother living in silence. And it's for Sting, who I banished from my life and my heart.

19

STING

The glass is cool against my forehead. Rain lashes the windowpane, blurring my view into Liberty's apartment. I don't use the binoculars tonight. I haven't since she cast me out of her life.

She wants her privacy, and I'll give it to her. But I won't stop watching. I won't stop watching her dark apartment, hoping for a sign, a signal that may never come.

Through the rain I can make out a soft glow coming from her apartment. The bathroom window remains dark, but the kitchen has a light on, and I imagine Liberty making dinner with classical music playing in the background, getting on with her normal life. Without me in it.

My heart constricts, and I clutch my chest, the pain so physical that I wonder if I'm having a heart attack. I may as well be. Without Liberty in my life, I've got nothing.

I should pack up. I should get out of this town. But I can't leave her. Not yet.

Movement across the darkness catches my eye, and I squint into the rain.

There's a flicker of light from her bathroom window. I

peer into the darkness, but the rain is too heavy. I can't be sure of what I'm seeing.

Grabbing the binoculars, I focus on her bathroom window.

Breaking up the darkness is the flickering light of a single candle.

My breath hitches. She remembers. She remembers what I told her about the candle, to light one in the window and those you love will find their way back.

I mentioned it a couple of times over the past few weeks when we were in the bath together. I couldn't tell her about my apartment looking into hers, but I hoped she'd know what to do if she ever needed me.

Liberty needs me.

I drop the binoculars and go to her.

A few minutes later, I ring the door to Liberty's apartment, then knock on the wooden frame impatiently.

When she opens it, my heart catches in my throat. She's beautiful, my angel, with her hair piled onto her head and her troubled eyes.

"You came," she whispers.

I step forward and take her in my arms. "I'll always come for you. Always."

She softens against my body, and I know she's mine. I scoop her into my arms and carry her to the living room.

"I need to tell you something, Sting."

My body stiffens, afraid of what she's going to say.

"I'm glad you killed my father." Her voice is a whisper, her eyes round with her confession. "It set me free."

Liberty fills me in on what her father did to her and her mother. By the time she gets to the trafficking of women, I'm pacing the room with my fists clenched.

The thought of him hurting Liberty makes me want to kill him all over again.

"I'm sorry for what he did to you."

Her hands tug at my shoulders, and I stop pacing.

"I know you've done some dark things, Sting. But I know you're not a bad man like he was."

She presses her cheek to my chest, and I put an arm around her. She's right. I have done some dark deeds, but I'd never hurt a woman.

"I love you, Sting. I want to be with you."

The words are a balm to my soul. My angel has come back to me.

I kiss the top of her head.

"Before I met you, I was an animal. You make me a better person, Liberty. You make me a better man."

She tilts her head back to look at me, and I press my lips to hers. Her warmth goes through me, warming my heart and my soul.

I feel a dark weight lift off my shoulders. She'll never know how she saved me, my angel, how her goodness made me a better person.

My real life starts now. It starts with Liberty. It's a life of hope, of promise—everything I never thought I deserved. It's a life where I can be a better man.

EPILOGUE

LIBERTY

Five years later…

I slide into the lavender-scented water, letting the warmth soak through to my bones.

There's a knot of anticipation in my stomach as I wait for the sound of the door opening that will signal Sting's arrival home.

The kids are with my mom for the weekend, and I'm starting Friday night off as I mean to continue. Naked in the bath, waiting for my husband.

While I wait for Sting, I drop a generous dollop of body wash onto a sponge and lather it over my body, spreading the foam up my arms and over my breasts, taking my time around my nipples, which are pebbled in anticipation.

I slide the sponge down my stomach, lovingly soaping the folds of my belly. This body has carried two children into existence, and I'm hoping there'll be another one soon. Saying a silent thank you to my body, I move the sponge between my legs.

My head tilts backward and my eyes drop closed as a sweet sensation courses through my body. A moan escapes my lips.

"Save some of that for me."

My eyes flick open, startled by Sting's voice. He's leaning against the door frame, watching me, his gaze intense.

"I didn't hear you come in."

He saunters over to the tub and plants a kiss on my lips.

"Surprise."

He takes the sponge out of my hand and runs it over my body, taking his time on my tits until my nipples are humming.

My husband doesn't talk much. He doesn't need to. And if he slips into the house without me hearing, I know it's a hangover from his old job.

We bought a nice house on the edge of town with space for our family and the foster children that come through. We're in the process of adopting two brothers who are in need of their forever home. At this rate, we'll soon need a bigger place to fit our quickly growing family.

Sting opened a shooting range, putting his skills to good use by offering shooting lessons and a place for gun enthusiasts to practice their skills.

If I wake in the night and he's not there, I don't ask questions. I know he doesn't work for Damon anymore, but I also know he'll never stop his own private war on drugs.

If he comes home in the night with a grim look on his face and a few less bullets in his bag, I feel proud that my husband is helping rid the world of those who would harm others.

He made peace with Damon, who gave us his blessing and a generous wedding gift. His funding still keeps the grief center open, and I've expanded it to offer more free sessions and take on other counselors.

I worked through my own issues with therapy and realized it doesn't matter if I haven't experienced grief myself. I can still help people deal with theirs.

Sting dips the sponge under the water, and I moan as he rubs it against my core. His shirt's getting wet, but he doesn't care. His focus is on me. I revel in it.

I let him rub and tease and push until he drives me over the edge, gripping the side of the bath as I come.

When I open my eyes, Sting is undressing. The candlelight throws his body into harsh shadows, accentuating every crevice, the burn scars, the army wounds—every mark on his body that tells the story of who he is. The neglected boy, the army hero, the hitman. My husband.

Sting sinks into the bath behind me, and I lean against him. His solid body feels reassuring behind me.

There's a hardness pressing into my back, and I rub against it, liking the way I can make him groan.

My pussy's throbbing from my orgasm. I turn around, needing more from him.

Rising onto my knees, I straddle Sting in the tub. I'm glad we got the extra-large tub in our ensuite. I love soaking in it after work, but I also love playing in it with my husband.

He slaps a hand on either side of my hips and I rise up, feeling powerful above him.

His cock floats to the top of the water, and I lower myself onto it, taking my time, letting him gently graze my opening.

We don't speak as I sink onto him.

Sting doesn't talk much, and I've learned to accept it. Instead, we communicate in other ways. The brush of his fingers on my throat shows me the gentleness he feels for me. The bite on my neck shows his desire.

As he lifts me up and down his cock, his teeth grazing my nipple, it conveys all the feeling I need, all the love that passes between us.

I feel his love in the intensity of his gaze as we release together. Sharing each other, coming together, our bodies and worlds colliding.

We don't need to talk. There are other ways to express love, and Sting knows them all.

SUNSET COAST TRILOGY

Read the other books in the Fletcher Family series.

The Thief's Lover tells the story of Chastity and Will and is a partners in crime, curvy girl romance with a hint of darkness and a whole lot of steam.

mybook.to/TheThiefsLover

The Henchman's Obsession tells Trinity and Karl's story. A stalker romance featuring an OTT alpha male and the curvy virgin he becomes obsessed with.

mybook.to/TheHenchmansObsession

Keep reading for an exclusive preview…

THE HENCHMAN'S OBSESSION

PROLOGUE

They call him a lot of things: heartless, poverty maker, the most hated man on the Sunset Coast. But they hardly ever call him Father.

The worn-looking man sitting behind the mahogany desk in a rumpled shirt with dark shadows under his eyes and a hand that trembles as he reaches for his whiskey glass is what most people don't see. Damon Fletcher—the father who's been broken by the disappearance of his daughters.

"She ran away three days ago, right after her sister."

I steal a glance at the man standing next to me, wondering why we've both been called in to hear this news.

I've not seen him before, but then again I don't know all of Damon's crew down the coast.

The one standing next to me is a huge brick of a man, with shoulders even wider than mine, a thickset jaw, eyes like pools of darkness, and a stillness about him that's unnerving.

He's staring straight ahead, his face passive, unmoved by the display of fatherly distress in front of us.

I've been working for Damon for six years, and I've never seen him like this.

My expertise lies in managing his interests further up the coast, doing what's necessary to keep his interests running and profitable.

Yesterday he called me down to the Sunset Coast to see him. It's not often I get called in by the boss.

"You think they're together?" I ask.

Damon brings the whiskey glass to his lips, takes a sip, then knocks it down in one gulp. His mouth puckers briefly, then he smacks his lips.

"No."

Being located up the coast, I've never met Damon's family, but I hear he's got two spoiled brats for daughters.

"Chastity will be fine." He sets his tumbler on the table and leans back in his chair. "But Trinity…"

Damon's eyes go misty, and for a frightful moment I think he's going to cry. I look at the beefcake next to me, but he's not giving anything away, the hardnosed bastard.

"Chastity is independent. She can look after herself. But Trinity is a sensitive soul. The thought of her being out there alone…"

He trails off, unable to go on.

It's hard to keep the irritation from my expression. She's probably partying it up with some preppy kid, spending her allowance on cocktails and tequila shots.

But I don't let the boss see what I'm thinking. No way.

"I'm sorry, sir."

"I want you to find her."

He leans on the table, and his eyes are suddenly sharp. His beady gaze lingers on mine and then shifts to the lump of man next to me.

I dig my nails into my palms, hoping he can't see my knuckles turning white. It doesn't pay to get angry with the boss. But I am angry. I've been brought down here away from my work to find some runaway rich girl who's probably shacked up with a trust fund baby enjoying a few days of freedom.

"Why us?"

I keep my voice steady, hoping I don't sound too petulant, but I feel fucking petulant. I'm a hard negotiator. I've got good business sense. Yet I'm being put to use tracking down a runaway. Not the best use of my skills.

"Because she doesn't know either of you."

Great. The out of town dudes get to do the babysitting. Beefcake still isn't saying anything, and I wonder if he's as pissed about this as I am.

"You think she doesn't want to be found?"

"I know she doesn't. She left this note."

Damon pulls a scribbled piece of paper out of a folder and lays it on the table. The writing is cursive, pretty with feminine curls to the letters.

I want a different life.
Don't try to find me.
Sorry, Daddy.

I wonder how long she'll last when she finds out that a different life doesn't involve all expenses paid by Daddy.

"Can't you track her credit card?" I ask.

"She didn't take it."

That surprises me. A rich-girl runaway isn't going to get far with no money.

"She withdrew a thousand dollars from the bank and left her card with the note. She could be anywhere."

Maybe she's found herself a sugar daddy to pay her way and give her the luxuries that I'm sure Damon's family must be used to.

I keep my thoughts to myself because suggesting to the boss that his daughter is likely hooking up with a rich older man who's demanding God knows what favors to keep her in luxury is likely to get me killed.

"I want you to work together to find her and bring her home."

"I work alone."

So, the beefcake speaks. The hard-ass next to me is staring intently at Damon. I don't like the thought of working with this guy either. I doubt there'd be many laughs with someone who has a permanent don't-fuck-with-me look etched on his face.

"That's fine with me. If you've got it covered, I'm not needed."

I raise my hands as if to concede, but Damon turns his gaze to me.

"Not so fast. Sting is an excellent tracker, but this requires a bit more sensitivity than what he's used to."

My mind reels at the name. Sting. The man's got quite a reputation.

The right hand of Damon. The man who does the deeds Damon doesn't want to dirty his hands with. There's a joke amongst us henchmen that if you go against the boss, he'll send Sting for you. The guy's a hitman.

"I work alone."

Sting says it again as if Damon hasn't just spoken. His voice chills me. No sane father would send this man after his little girl.

But when has Damon Fletcher ever been sane?

"You work together."

Damon counters Sting casually as if he's a wayward child that needs pulling into line and not a massive fucking scary as shit hitman.

Sting still doesn't move, and I wonder if that's something he learned in hitman training, how to stay really fucking still and freak everyone the fuck out.

Damon pulls a photo out of his folder and throws it on the table.

"This is Trinity."

My gaze goes to the image, and my heart stops. There's a ringing in my ears, and everything blurs around me, except that photo.

The picture's taken on a boat, the family yacht no doubt. A young woman, Trinity, sits side-on to the camera, her shoulders twisted frontward, laughing at something just out of frame.

She's wearing a sheer wrap thrown over her bikini-clad shoulders, the lines of her cleavage visible under the fabric. Her head's thrown back in a laugh that shows off plump lips, straight teeth, and her pink tongue poking over her bottom teeth. Smile lines draw attention to her sparkling eyes that are the same color as the water around the boat.

Her neck is elongated, and there's a sprinkling of freckles on her nose and throat.

She's beautiful, more than beautiful. There's a pull to her, a stirring in my gut telling me that this woman is my destiny.

Mine.

A possessiveness grabs my heart, and I know without a doubt that my life will never be the same again.

Damon's talking, but I don't hear what he's saying. My eyes are transfixed on Trinity's face, committing it to memory. Her image is branded into my heart.

Mine.

The world swims around my mind, and I feel dizzy. I need to find this woman. For my own sanity, I need to find her and make her mine.

"I'll find her." My voice comes out as a croak. "I don't need Sting."

Damon peers at me, and I wonder if he can sense what just happened, how my whole world just shifted.

"I'll do it alone."

Damon looks between us, exasperated like we're his naughty children who won't play ball. But Sting only works alone, and I don't want anyone cramping my style.

"Fine," he says. "Find her, Karl. Find her and bring her home."

"Yes, sir."

I'll find her, all right. I'll bring her home. Home to me, where she belongs.

> To keep reading visit:
> mybook.to/TheHenchmansObsession

BOOKS BY SADIE KING

Series set on the Sunset Coast
Men of the Sea
Sunset Security
Underground Crows MC
The Thief's Lover

Series set in Maple Springs
Men of Maple Mountain
All the Single Dads
Candy's Café
Small Town Sisters

Series set in Kings County
Kings of Fire
King's Cops

For more of Sadie King's books check out her website
www.authorsadieking.com

ABOUT THE AUTHOR

Sadie King is a USA Today Best Selling Author of short instalove romance.
She lives in New Zealand with her ex-military husband and raucous young son.

Follow Sadie King on BookBub to get an alert whenever she has a new release, preorder, or discount!

www.bookbub.com/authors/sadie-king

www.authorsadieking.com

GET YOUR FREE BOOK

Sign up to the Sadie King mailing list for a FREE book!

You'll be the first to hear about exclusive offers, bonus content and all the news from Sadie King.

To claim your free book visit:
www.authorsadieking.com/free

Printed in Great Britain
by Amazon